NICK JR. **Little Bill** ®

Is It My Turn Now?

by Catherine Lukas
illustrated by Bernie Cavender

SCHOLASTIC INC.
New York Toronto London Auckland Sydney
Mexico City New Delhi Hong Kong Buenos Aires

ISBN 0-439-66677-5

12 11 10 9 8 7 6 5 4 3 2 1   4 5 6 7 8 9/0

Printed in the U.S.A.

First Scholastic printing, September 2004

"Mmmm! Those cookies smell good!" said Little Bill, racing into the kitchen. "Can I have one?"

"Nope," April said. "These are for my bake sale."

"Oh," said Little Bill. "Do you want to play space explorers with me?"

"Maybe later, Little Bill," she said, grabbing her jacket. "I have a game. See you there in a little while!"

As April hurried out, Little Bill went into the living room to play by himself.

Little Bill took out his space toys and was soon in battle.

"Aliens attacking!" Little Bill cried. "Raise the shields and prepare for—"

"Come on, Little Bill, we have to hurry," said his mother, Brenda. "The last batch of cookies is finally done, and we're late for April's game."

Little Bill put down his spaceship with a sigh. "I was just about to save the universe," he said, following his mother out the door.

April's game was exciting. In the final minute the score was tied.
Then *swish!* April hit a shot at the buzzer!

"Hooray!" yelled Little Bill.

The whole family headed down to see her, but Little Bill couldn't get close to her. She was surrounded by a crowd of people.

"Good game, April!" said Little Bill. But April didn't hear him.

The next day Little Bill was watching Captain Brainstorm on TV.
It was the show's final moments. "You did it again, Captain Brainstorm!"
Little Bill cheered.

"Little Bill," said his father, Big Bill. "We need to get going.
Bobby's chess match starts in fifteen minutes."

"But I have to stay for the end of the show!" Little Bill cried.

Big Bill sat down next to Little Bill. "I know you want to keep watching, Sport, but this is Bobby's big day. We need to be there for him."

Little Bill sighed. "Okay," he said, as his father turned off the television.

The chess match was close. Bobby was doing great. Little Bill watched his big brother move the piece shaped like a horse's head. He began to imagine himself in an exciting chess match.

"Don't worry, Queen!" cried Sir Bill, the knight. "I'll protect you!"

He galloped over to her square and bowed.

"Shhhhh!" Little Bill heard someone say.

"Sorry," he muttered, and sat back down in his chair.

When he got home later that afternoon Little Bill stomped into his room and sat down on his bed. "Everyone is so busy around here," he told Elephant.

But Elephant didn't look up. He was exercising on his wheel.

"Elephant, are you too busy to play with me too?" Little Bill asked.

At school the next day Miss Murray made an announcement. "We are going to put on a play," she told the class. "Each of you will be responsible for making your own costume and for remembering your lines."

Miss Murray had a script for each person in the class. "Here you are, Little Bill," she said, handing him a script with his name on it. "You are going to be a walrus."

"A *walrus*?" Little Bill repeated.

Back at home that afternoon Little Bill sat down at the kitchen table and sighed.

"What's the matter, Little Bill?" asked Alice the Great. She stopped what she was doing and sat down next to him.

Little Bill took the crumpled script out of his jacket pocket and handed it to her. "I'm in a play," he said. "I'm supposed to be a walrus, but I don't even know what color walruses are or what they sound like!"

"Well!" Alice the Great replied. "We'll help you figure it out. That's what families do. They help each other."

"Come on, Little Bill," said Bobby, hopping to his feet. "Let's go find some pictures of walruses on the computer."

The next day Alice the Great showed Little Bill fabric she had bought. "I think this will make a very nice walrus costume, Little Bill."

"Cool!" Little Bill shouted. The fabric looked brown and wrinkly, just like a walrus's skin.

"Hey, I have an idea!" said April. "Why don't we go to the zoo tomorrow? We can visit the walruses and see what kind of noise they make!"

"Great idea, honey," said Brenda. "Why don't we all go?"

"Don't you guys have a whole bunch of other things you need to do?" Little Bill asked.

"You are number one on the family's list right now, Little Bill," said Big Bill with a grin.

They spent a lot of time watching the walruses at the zoo.

"Do you know your lines yet, Little Bill?" asked April.

"Yup! I get to bark like a walrus!" he said cheerfully.

"Bark! Bark!"

"Let's practice together," said Big Bill. As the two of them barked,
all of the walruses seemed to join in!

The day of the play Little Bill's family was very proud. When Miss Murray got to the part about the walrus, Little Bill remembered his line: "Bark! Bark!" he yelled out as loudly as he could.

At the end of the play the audience gave the class a standing ovation.

"It sure was a busy day today," Little Bill said to Elephant at bedtime that night. "First we had to pick up Bobby, then we all went to my play, and then we had to take April to practice. But don't worry, Elephant. No matter how busy I get, I'll always make time to play with you. You're part of our family!"